Princess
Bing Bong
Rides A Bike

VANESSA PANICCIA

Illustrated by Susan Shorter

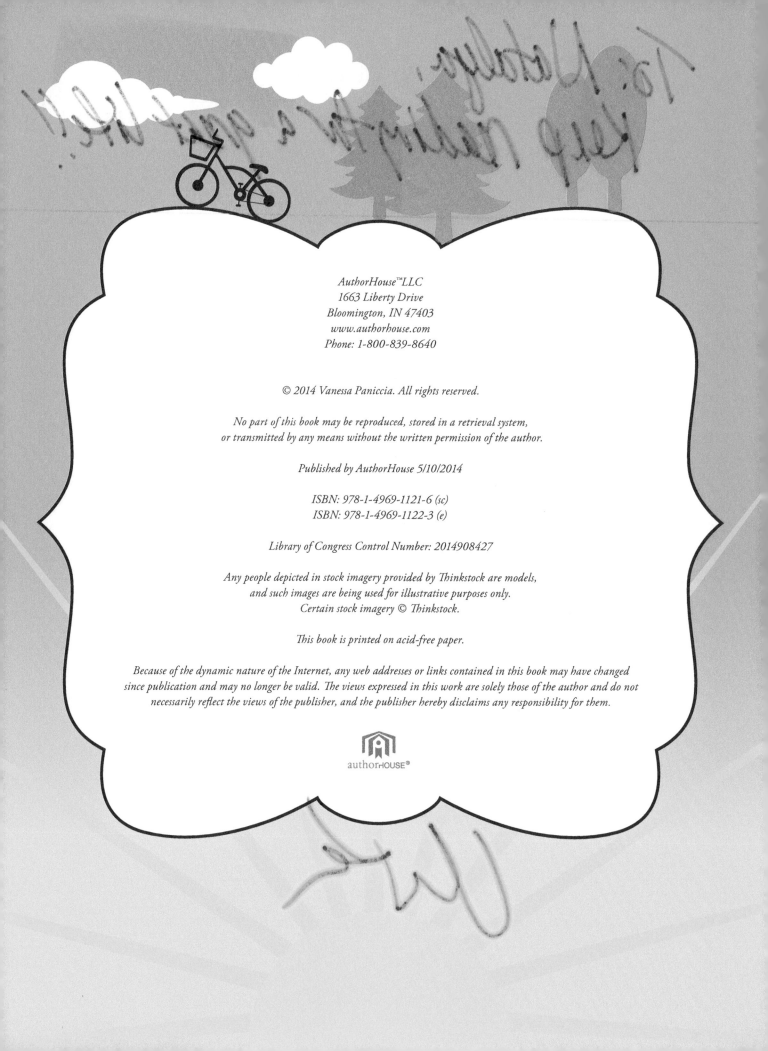

AuthorHouse™ LLC
1663 Liberty Drive
Bloomington, IN 47403
www.authorhouse.com
Phone: 1-800-839-8640

Published by AuthorHouse 5/10/2014

ISBN: 978-1-4969-1121-6 (sc)
ISBN: 978-1-4969-1122-3 (e)

Library of Congress Control Number: 2014908427

Any people depicted in stock imagery provided by Thinkstock are models,
and such images are being used for illustrative purposes only.
Certain stock imagery © Thinkstock.

This book is printed on acid-free paper.

Because of the dynamic nature of the Internet, any web addresses or links contained in this book may have changed
since publication and may no longer be valid. The views expressed in this work are solely those of the author and do not
necessarily reflect the views of the publisher, and the publisher hereby disclaims any responsibility for them.

authorHOUSE®

Princess Bing Bong was excited about her new bike.
It had sparkly training wheels, purple racing stripes,
and a glittery basket up front for her pet stuffed monkey Gibbles.
There was only one problem....
Princess Bing Bong did not know how to ride a bike.

One fine, sunny day, Princess Bing Bong's father,
King Flapjack took Princess Bing Bong out
for her first bike riding lesson.
She couldn't wait to ride her fast bike!
She was going to be faster than an airplane,
a rocket ship, and definitely faster than everyone at her school!

With her pet stuffed monkey Gibbles tucked safely in her basket
and her new gorilla helmet on,
Princess Bing Bong was ready for action!
"Oh no, here we go", sighed Gibbles.
He was afraid they were headed for trouble like they usually were.

8

With a gentle push from King Flapjack,
Princess Bing Bong started pedaling down the path.
She was riding!!
Then she forgot to pedal.
She couldn't remember how to get her feet back on the pedals.
"Put your feet to the pedals!" called King Flapjack
The bike kept going and Princess Bing Bong was panicked.
She couldn't remember what to do so she held
the handlebars and stuck her feet in the air.

Princess Bing Bong was headed towards a big hill.
She was going faster and faster
and Gibbles was hiding as far down in the basket as he could.
Princess Bing Bong could see the farmer's market down below the hill
with all of the farmers selling fruits and vegetables.

"Oh no! Not again!" shouted Gibbles.
With a crash, a bang, and a boom,
Princess Bing Bong and Gibbles
crashed into Mr. Scowl's lemon and lime stand.
The fruit went flying everywhere!

"I never, ever, ever, EVER, want to ride my bike again,"
sighed Princess Bing Bong.
Princess Bing Bong forgot that most people do not fly down hills
and land in fruit stands.
Gibbles was pretty sure that Princess Bing Bong
was the only person that has ever done that.

The next morning, Princess Bing Bong woke up to King Flapjack holding her gorilla bicycle helmet.

"Time to wake up for your second lesson,"
announced King Flapjack

"What if I land in a fruit stand?" asked Princess Bing Bong

"You won't", replied King Flapjack

"What if I hit a tree?" asked Princess Bing Bong

"You won't", responded King Flapjack

"What if I fall down?" asked Princess Bing Bong

"You will, I still do, but you'll get back up and be fine,"
answered King Flapjack

With a little nudge from her father,
Princess Bing Bong was off and she was pedaling all by herself.
She got nervous and took her feet off the pedals.
She wobbled.
She put her feet back on the pedals.
She took her feet off.
The bike wiggled.

Off in the distance, Princess Bing Bong spotted her best friends
riding bikes in a big crowd of people.
Princess Bing Bong rode as fast as she could to try
to catch up to join them.

Before she knew it, she was on the racetracks.
She was pedaling so fast, she didn't even notice that
her training wheels had come off.
Princess Bing Bong was on two wheels!
She was determined to catch up.

Everyone had numbers on their shirts
and the crowd was screaming her name wildly.
Someone had put a number on Princess Bing Bong's shirt.
"I think we're in a race, Gibbles," shouted Princess Bing Bong.
"Let's ride!"

Princess Bing Bong rode faster than she ever thought possible.
She couldn't believe it when she was the first one to ride
through the giant red ribbon at the end of the race.
A lady handed her the biggest trophy she had ever seen!
Queen Mumbles gave Princess Bing Bong a giant hug!
She was so proud. Princess Bing Bong thought,
" This is the best day of my whole life!"

Queen Mumbles carried an exhausted Princess Bing Bong,
her bike, and Gibbles home.
Princess Bing Bong really could ride a bike.
She just had to remember to be brave.

CPSIA information can be obtained at www.ICGtesting.com
Printed in the USA
BVOW10s1152180514

353802BV00003B/8/P

Princess Bing Bong is overly excited to try out her She doesn't know how to ride it yet but she imagines that she will be very fast. Bike riding lessons don't start out so well but Princess Bing Bong learns that she can accomplish anything with a little perseverance. Never give up, dreams do come true!

Vanessa Paniccia has enjoyed decades of writing, reading, and storytelling. An avid teller of fantastical stories with unusual and interesting characters, sure to entertain and surprise all ages. She resides in Rhode Island with her husband and three young children.

authorHOUSE®

ISBN 978-1-4969-1121-6

51899

9 781496 911216

THEMATIC UNIT

OUR ENVIRONMENT

TCM 272

Reproducible   Primary

- **Literature-Based**   • **Across the Curriculum**   • **Cooperative Learning**

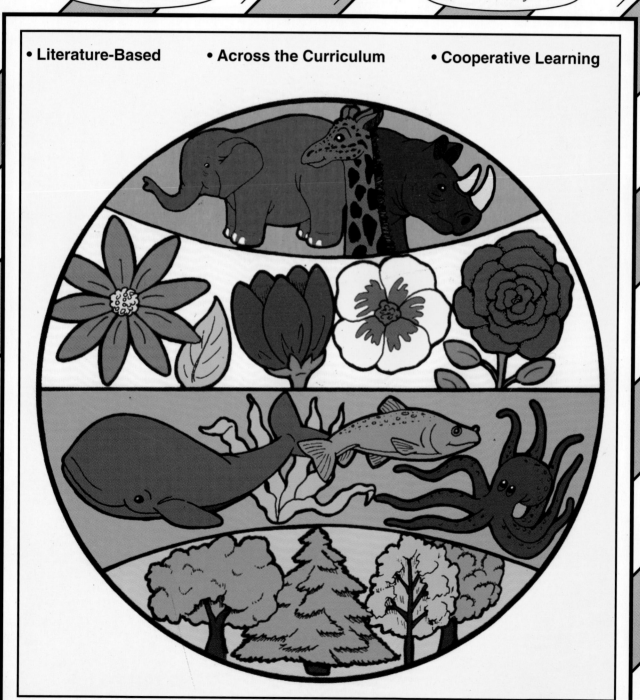

Teacher Created Materials, Inc.

Literature-Based Thematic Units

EARLY CHILDHOOD
TCM250—Animals
TCM253—Community Workers
TCM2110—Families
TCM2059—Farm
TCM584—My Body
TCM252—My World
TCM244—Plants
TCM255—Safety
TCM254—Sea Animals
TCM251—Seasons
TCM2111—Things That Go

PRIMARY
TCM2113—Ants
TCM266—Apples
TCM267—Bears
TCM256—Birds
TCM264—Birthdays
TCM275—Bubbles
TCM2118—Chocolate
TCM259—Christmas
TCM279—Color
TCM268—Creepy Crawlies
TCM271—Dragons & Dinosaurs
TCM261—Easter & St. Patrick's Day
TCM246—Fairy Tales
TCM270—Five Senses
TCM278—Food
TCM274—Friendship
TCM2112—Grandparents
TCM257—Halloween
TCM2117—Ice Cream
TCM586—My Country
TCM276—Native Americans
TCM272—Our Environment
TCM248—Peace
TCM277—Penguins
TCM263—Popcorn
TCM262—Presidents' Day & Martin Luther King, Jr. Day
TCM2116—Quilts
TCM2114—Rivers & Ponds
TCM265—Rocks & Soil
TCM269—Self-Esteem
TCM258—Thanksgiving
TCM249—Tide Pools & Coral Reefs
TCM260—Valentine's Day
TCM273—Weather

INTERMEDIATE
TCM239—Chocolate
TCM593—Cowboys
TCM238—Dinosaurs
TCM286—Ecology
TCM236—Electricity
TCM281—Flight
TCM280—Friends
TCM240—Geology
TCM241—Gold Rush
TCM235—The Human Body
TCM589—Ice Cream
TCM234—Immigration
TCM592—Insects
TCM232—Inventions
TCM283—Jungle
TCM237—Money
TCM230—Multicultural Folk Tales
TCM285—Native Americans
TCM284—Oceans
TCM233—Peace
TCM460—Quilts
TCM587—Space
TCM591—Spiders
TCM588—Sports
TCM242—Tall Tales
TCM231—Water
TCM282—Westward Ho

CHALLENGING
TCM590—African Americans
TCM292—Ancient Egypt
TCM297—Ancient Greece
TCM596—Ancient Rome
TCM296—Archaeology
TCM461—Chocolate
TCM290—Civil War
TCM597—Colonial America
TCM288—Explorers
TCM210—Holocaust
TCM294—Industrial Revolution

TCM595—Mayans, Aztecs and Incas
TCM291—Medieval Times
TCM580—Renaissance
TCM293—Revolutionary War
TCM295—Transcontinental Railroad
TCM582—U.S. Constitution
TCM599—Vietnam War
TCM583—Wolves
TCM598—World War I
TCM581—World War II

Watch for additional titles from

Teacher Created Materials

Teacher Created Materials